BLACK SAND BEACH

ARE YOU AFRAID OF THE LIGHT?

BY RICHARD FAIRGRAY

PIXEL
+INK

For Dasher

Pixel+Ink Books

Text and illustrations copyright © 2020 by Richard Fairgray
All Rights Reserved
Pixel+Ink is a division of Trustbridge Development Corp.
Printed and bound in 2020 at Tien Wah Press, Malaysia.
Book design by Richard Fairgray
www.pixelandinkbooks.com
First Edition
1 3 5 7 9 10 8 6 4 2

Library of Congress Cataloging-in-Publication Data is available upon request.

HI, DASH. HI, LILY.

GEE, DASH. BRING ENOUGH WITH YA?

HI, MR. WEST.

HI, MRS. AUSTEN *HYPHEN* WEST!

SERIOUSLY, SON, DID YOU LEAVE *ANYTHING* BEHIND?

IT'S MOSTLY *BOOKS*.

IN CASE I TURN OUT TO BE *RIGHT* AND THE OUTDOORS REALLY IS TERRIBLE.

AND *HERE* I WAS WORRIED IT WAS FULL OF *HAIR* PRODUCTS.

JUST THREE BOTTLES.

GREAT.

HOPE YOU PACKED THEM AT THE *TOP* OF THE SUITCASE.

SQUELCH

BLACK SAND BEACH, HERE WE *COME!*

I *HEARD* THAT THE *CARNIVAL'S* COMING TO TOWN AND THAT THEY HAVE A SLIDE SO *BIG* YOU HAVE TO TAKE *TWO* ELEVATORS TO GET TO THE *TOP* AND THEN SIX FLIGHTS OF STAIRS TO GET BACK *DOWN* WHEN YOU REALIZE IT'S TOO *SCARY*.

LUCKY US, *WE'LL* BE AT THE BEACH.

UH-HUH.

IT *MIGHT* NOT BE AS BAD AS YOU *THINK*. YOU HAVEN'T BEEN THERE SINCE YOU WERE WHAT, *SIX*?

LILY, YOU DON'T *GET IT*. BLACK SAND BEACH ISN'T LIKE AN ORDINARY *BEACH*.

THERE'S *NO* ICE-CREAM STAND OR *STORES*, THERE'S JUST *GIANT* MOSQUITOES, *SCARY* WOODS, *WEIRD* ANIMALS AND A *SHAKY* OLD HOUSE THAT MY DAD BUILT HIMSELF.

YOU'VE SEEN MY DAD. HE BARELY LOOKS LIKE HE COULD BUILD A *SANDWICH*!

3

DASH, DID YOU TELL *LILY* WHY THEY CALL IT *BLACK SAND* BEACH?

IS IT BECAUSE THE *SAND* IS *BLACK*?

YUP.

BUT *NO ONE* KNOWS WHY THEY DECIDED TO *PAINT* IT!

THAT.

A *WHOLE SUMMER* OF JOKES THAT GOOD.

OKAY, *WINDOWS* UP.

WE'RE ABOUT TO HEAD INTO *MOSQUITO* GULCH.

MOSQUITO GULCH

THIS IS THEIR WORLD. YOU'RE
JUST DRIVIN' THROUGH IT.

I *SWEAR* THEY GET BIGGER EVERY YEAR.

MOLCHUK

UHH

STAY AWAY FROM THAT *HOUSE*.

THEY'RE-

THAT FAMILY JUST AIN'T RIGHT.

THEN *BUZZ BUZZ BUZZ BUZZ BUZZ BUZZ BUZZ BUZZ BUZZ!*

I *FOUND* THEM IN A *TREE* AND THE BUZZING WAS SO NICE—

BUT *THEN* I WAS DOING BIG *FARTS* ON HER PILLOW BECAUSE I FORGOT ALL ABOUT ALL THE BEES—

SO, I *HID* THEM IN HER PILLOW SO SHE *WOULDN'T KNOW.*

BUT *ELEANOR* HAD SAID NO MORE *BEES* IN THE *HOUSE* BECAUSE OF ALL THE OTHER TIMES—

PHEWPH!

SO, *THAT'S* MY COUSIN ANDY.

AND *THAT* IS MY COUSIN ELEANOR.

DASH?!

HEY, CUZ!

TOO TIGHT. TOO TIGHT.

RIGHT, YOU JUST GOT HERE, SO MY MOM LIKE *JUST* PUNCHED YOU, RIGHT?

SHE'S *SO* LAME.

SHE DOES THAT TO EVERYONE.

HI, I'M ELEANOR, DASH'S *FULLY* MATURE AND GROWN UP *COUSIN*. WELCOME TO THE MONKEY HOUSE.

I'M *LILY*, LILY POWERS. WOW.

DASH, HOW CAN YOU NOT *LOVE* THIS PLACE? IT HAS *EVERYTHING!*

THE *HOUSE* IS ON *POLES.* YOUR *AUNT* RIDES A *ZOMBIE SHEEP.* YOUR COUSIN OWNS HIS OWN *BEES.*

THE *WHOLE* PLACE IS LIKE A CRAZY TREE FORT AND—

UMM.

THAT'S UNCLE FREDERICK. HE'S JUST *VERY* QUIET.

OK, BUT IT'S STILL *MOSTLY AWESOME!*

IS *EVERY-BODY* PAYING ATTENTION?

OKAY, *THESE* ARE THE *RULES* OF *BLACK SAND* BEACH.

NUMBER ONE—

WHOA! HOW ARE YOU *DOING THAT?* YOU DIDN'T EVEN *TOUCH* THE SAND?

OH, THAT'S EASY. IT'S *MAGNETS*.

... THE SAND AROUND HERE HAS SO MUCH IRON IN IT THAT IT'S ALL *MAGNETIC*.

CHECK IT.

THE *BIGGER* THE MAGNET, THE MORE *SAND* YOU CAN MOVE.

TRY IT.

OKAY, BACK TO THE *RULES*.

NEVER GET CAUGHT BY THE *TIDE*.

NEVER GO IN THE BUSH IF IT'S DARK.

YOU LISTENING, LILY?

YEAH, STAY OUT OF THE BUSH AT NIGHT. *GOT IT.*

NO!

NOT JUST AT *NIGHT*.

STAY OUT OF THEM IN THE *DARK!*

WOW, YOUR *COUSIN* IS REALLY COOL.

YEAH, SHE IS. I *SOMETIMES* WONDER HOW THE REST OF THE FAMILY IS ALL SO WEIRD.

NO, I MEANT *ANDY*. I MEAN, ELEANOR'S COOL TOO, BUT-

I THINK-

I THINK HE MIGHT BE A *GENIUS*.

WHAT?

HE ONCE ACCIDENTALLY ATE *ROCKS* FOR BREAKFAST!

It's weird being back here after this much time. I haven't been here since I was six, but it all just feels so familiar. Andy is still exactly the same as I remember. Mom used to say he was "made of chaos," which I guess is sort of true.

Today he tried to fly with a backpack full of bees. I don't think I've ever known someone to have a backpack full of bees.

Eleanor is still cooler and smarter than any of us, which will probably get pretty annoying soon.

Aunt Lynne isn't as fun as I remember. Like, her picking on dad and acting like one of the kids used to be funny, but now she just seems like an annoying little sister, even to me.

Here's the weirdest thing, though. I can't figure out how I know this place so well.

Like, it's a family beach house and I know I've been here before, but not for a really long time. I think the last time I was here I was only six, but it just feels like home.

This place is weird and it's making me feel weird.

I thought I heard someone whispering my name today at the beach.

Not a person.

Like, it was coming from the ocean.
I sound insane.

DDDDAAAAASSSSSHHHHHHHH.

BUT, THEY *WERE* FROM A CHICKEN *ORIGINALLY*, YES?

BEATS ME!

I HEAR YA, UNCLE FRED.

SO, I THOUGHT WE COULD TAKE THE *BOOGIE BOARDS* OUT TO THE SAND DUNES TODAY AND GO *SLIDING*!

I *THINK* I'll stay *HERE* and read my magazines.

THERE'S ENOUGH SAND INSIDE, AND IN MY *COFFEE* CUP FOR MY TASTES.

ACTUALLY, WE WERE GOING TO GO CHECK OUT SOME STUFF THIS MORNING. JUST US KIDS.

GREAT, I'LL COME TOO!

FORGET IT, *DALE*. WE'RE FIXING THAT *DOOR* TODAY!

ONE O' YOUR LOT *FELL* THROUGH IT I *THINK*.

PLEASE DON'T LEAVE ME ALONE WITH HER.

I *WANNA* SLIDE!

<SIGH>

FUMMP

SMOOTH.

ELEANOR, I NEED TO *ASK* YOU SOMETHING.

GO FOR IT.

YOU SAID THE *LIGHTHOUSE* DOESN'T WORK.

UH-HUH.

BUT I *WOKE* UP LAST NIGHT AND—

THE LIGHT WAS ON.

WHERE?

THE *LIGHT* IN THE LIGHTHOUSE!

!

NO, WE DON'T NE-

ANDY, LILY, BRING IT IN!

GUYS, LISTEN. THERE'S-

UNCLE *DALE.*

UMM-

WE *NEED* TO DROP YOU BACK AT THE *HOUSE.*

LISTEN, UNCLE DALE, WE NEED *YOU* ON A *SUPER SECRET* MISSION AT HOME BASE.

IF MY *MOM* FIXES THAT DOOR BY *HERSELF,* THERE'LL BE NO *TELLING* WHAT SHE'LL DO!

BUT-BUT-

WELL, IT *LOOKS* LIKE *NOBODY* HAS BEEN IN HERE IN A *VERY* LONG TIME.

SO, IF WE'RE THINKING *SOMEONE* WAS TURNING THE LIGHT ON—

DIDN'T YOU SAY THIS LIGHTHOUSE WAS FULLY *AUTOMATED*?

YEAH, BUT I ALSO SAID IT NEVER *WORKED* PROPERLY.

NOTHING HAS *MOVED* IN HERE IN YEARS.

EXCEPT THIS.

THE COBWEBS ARE EVERYWHERE EXCEPT ON THIS *POLE.*

I *THINK* THIS IS WHAT MAKES THE LIGHT TURN.

AND IT *LOOKS* LIKE IT'S BEEN *TURNING.*

I THINK WE'RE *TRAPPED*.

NO NO NO NO NO. THAT'S *IMPOSSIBLE*. HOW DID THE TIDE COME IN THAT *FAST*?

DASH, WE'LL BE FINE. WE JUST HAVE TO *WAIT A FEW* HOURS AND WE CAN WALK BACK.

FORGET IT.

NO *WAY* AM I WAITING HERE, WHERE WHATEVER IS DOING THIS *WANTS* US TO BE!

DAAASSSSHHH.

ANDY, *HOW* DID YOU GET SO MANY *EGGS* IN YOUR POCKETS?

WITH A FUNNEL.

OBVIOUSLY.

ANDY, YOU—

YOU ARE *SO* GROSS.

BUT THANKS FOR BRINGING *FOOD*.

ANYONE WANT TO HEAR ME *FART* THE ALPHABET?

KIND OF.

TO BE CONTINUED.

THE HAUNTED LIGHTHOUSE

PART 2

UMM . . .

OH NO! INVISIBLE GHOSTS!

NO, ANDY. JUST **NO** GHOSTS.

I **SWEAR**, GUYS. THE LIGHT WAS ON AND ALL **GREEN** AND THESE SHIPWRECKED PEOPLE WERE **FLOATING** UP TOWARD THE LIGHTHOUSE ASKING WHY **I** TURNED OUT THE **LIGHT!**

OHH, SO **YOU** TURNED OUT THE **LIGHT.**

DUDE, TURN IT BACK **ON** SO WE CAN SEE THE **GHOSTS!**

ANDY, I **DIDN'T** TURN OUT THE LIGHT, I–

NEVER MIND.

HUH.

OK, IS EVERY-
BODY OK?

YEAH.

YUP.

UH-HUH.

HMMM.

IT'S POINTING AT THE BEACH.

NOW THE WOODS.

OCEAN! IT'S ON THE WATER!

IS THERE ANY *FRESHER* FOOD?

BE GRATEFUL WHILE YOU GET THIS, **SHARON**.

WITH ALL YOU *EXTRAS* TURNIN' UP WE MIGHT HAVE TA DIG INTO THE **UNLABELED** CANS.

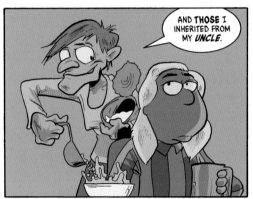

AND **THOSE** I INHERITED FROM MY *UNCLE*.

FLAKES, ELEANOR?

MORNIN', FREDERICK.

WHO WANTS TO HIKE UP TO *CELLPHONE* HILL TODAY?

I FIGURE WE ALL GO TOGETHER. GET IN SOME GOOD *QUANTITY* TIME AS A FAMILY.

SO, Y'KNOW, *FUN* . . . BUT MANDATORY.

BLASTED KNOTS.

WHAT'S CELLPHONE HILL?

ONLY PLACE ON THE PENINSULA THAT GETS CELL SERVICE.

WAITING ON A CALL, UNCLE DALE?

GO ON, DALE.

TELL 'EM WHY YOU'RE DRAGGIN' US UP THERE.

UHM. SHARON N-NEEDS TO CHECK UPS FAMILY AND . . .

PLACE SOME *ORDERS.*

SO, **SOMETHING**'S BEEN BOTHERING ME ABOUT LAST NIGHT.

UMM, *YEAH*, THE HORDES OF SHIPWRECKED GHOSTS TRYING TO *CLAW* OUR *FACES* OFF.

OH NO, ELEANOR! IS THAT WHAT HAPPENED TO YOUR *FACE*?

IT LOOKS *TERRIBLE!*

I THINK IT WAS THE *LIGHT-HOUSE*

UR, YES, THE GHOSTS.

BUT I DON'T THINK THEY WERE THE THING THAT WAS REALLY *AFTER* US.

THINK ABOUT IT, DID ANYONE EVEN GET *TOUCHED* BY ONE OF THE GHOSTS?

AND THE WAY THE *TIDE* SUDDENLY CAME IN TO TRAP US?

THE WAY THE *LIGHT MOVED*. THAT'S *NOT* HOW LIGHTHOUSES WORK.

THEY EITHER SWIVEL OR *BLINK* ON AND OFF. THAT ONE WAS . . .

WHAT DO YOU MEAN?

IT WAS LIKE IT WAS *LOOKING* FOR US.

I MEAN, I *DON'T* THINK THE GREEN LIGHT BROUGHT THE GHOSTS. *I THINK* IT JUST SHOWED US GHOSTS WE DON'T NORMALLY SEE.

OK, THIS IS SOUNDING A BIT–

AND WHAT'S *MORE*, I DON'T THINK WE DID ANYTHING TO REALLY *STOP* IT.

EXTENSION CORDS!

ANDY, YOU'RE A GENIUS!

SERIOUSLY, WHY DOES EVERYONE KEEP *SAYING* THAT? REMEMBER WHEN HE HUGGED THAT **CACTUS** BECAUSE IT WAS IN A *PRICKLY MOOD*?

ARE YOU QUITE FINISHED, **HARRY-GILBERT**?

EVERY **FALL** WHEN WE LEAVE HERE, THE MOLCHUKS BREAK IN AND RUN EXTENSION CORDS TO THEIR HOUSE TO **STEAL** OUR POWER.

AND EVERY **SUMMER**, MOM WINDS UP ALL THE CORDS AND **HIDES** THEM IN THE CRAWL SPACE.

THAT'S **PERFECT!** HOW MANY DO WE HAVE?

I MEASURED A COUPLE OF YEARS BACK.

IT'S ABOUT **FOUR MILES** WORTH.

HOME.

SM CK

LILY, THAT WAS SO *AWESOME!* YOU TOOK OUT *ONE* TINY COG AND THE *WHOLE THING* JUST STOPPED!

NO MORE CREEPY GREEN LIGHT, NO MORE *GHOSTS!*

DASH JUST STANDING THERE LIKE "DUR I AM A FROZEN ROBOT."

AND THEN THAT *SPARKY SNAKE* WAS THERE—

AND *BAM!*

LILY *SMACKS* HIM IN THE HEAD AND HE'S NOTHING BUT *DUST.*

YO, *DASH,* YOU GOIN' ALL WEIRDO ROBOT AGAIN?

SO YOU GUYS COULD SEE HIM . . . IT?

NO, **ANDY**. I'M FINE.

YEAH, *JUST* FOR A **SECOND**. IT WAS SO DARK THAT WE COULDN'T SEE YOU, AND YOU WEREN'T *ANSWERING* WHEN WE CALLED.

THEN LILY PULLED OUT THIS COG AND–

I DON'T KNOW. IT GOT *LIGHTER*.

AND YOU WERE JUST *STANDING* THERE STARING UP AT IT – THIS BIG, SPARKY **SNAKE** THING SO–

SO **BAM!**

LILY SMACKED HIM **DOWN**. SAVED THE DAY TWICE!

DASH?

YEAH.

I DIDN'T WANT TO MENTION IT IN FRONT OF THE **OTHERS,** BUT I—

IT **DID** SAY SOMETHING TO ME, LILY.

WHAT?

THE **SPARKY SNAKE.** IT SAID WE HAD A "CONNECTION" ME AND HIM. THAT I'D **REMEMBER** HIM.

WOW. THAT'S REALLY—

OK, I **HAVE** TO SHOW YOU SOMETHING.

WHAT IS IT?

THIS.

IT'S WHAT I *HIT* THE SNAKE WITH.

THAT'S ONE OF MY *JOURNALS!*

WHY DO–

I *DIDN'T* STEAL IT.

I UMM– I FOUND IT IN THE LIGHTHOUSE.

THAT'S **NOT** THE WEIRDEST PART.

LOOK AT THE DATES.

THIS IS– THIS IS MY JOURNAL FROM LAST SUMMER.

YEAH, AND *EVERY ENTRY* IN THERE IS ABOUT **BLACK SAND BEACH.**

YOU WERE *HERE* LAST SUMMER, DASH.

I *THOUGHT* YOU HADN'T BEEN HERE SINCE YOU WERE SIX.

SO DID I.

THEY'RE **READY.**

MONDAY

SO, DO WE *TELL* THE OTHERS ABOUT THE JOURNAL?

NOT YET. I WANT TO FIGURE OUT WHAT'S GOING ON FIRST.

I DON'T KNOW. THEY SEEM—

IF I REALLY *WAS* HERE LAST YEAR THEN *WHY* HAVEN'T THEY MENTIONED IT?

CAN ANDY AND ELEANOR BE *TRUSTED?*

OK, IT'S UP TO YOU, DASH.

THERE'S ONE OTHER THING.

GET YER *BUTTS* IN HERE, YOU TWO! WE GOT *FRESH PRODUCE!*

WE'RE IN FOR A TREAT TONIGHT. THEM BROTHERS UP AT THE FLECKOWITZ FARM ARE DOING THEIR *BIANNUAL CATTLE RELOCATION!*

FLECKOWITZ FARMS

CATTLE RELO-?

EVERY season they have to move the **COWS** from up the hill to the valley, and the **STAMPEDE** goes right under this house.

UH-HUH. So every time they give us a *BIG BOX* of **THANK-YOU FOOD** and we eat fresh for th'night.

PEOPLE said it was a *DUMB* reason to build the house on this spot, but I betcha *THEY* don't get free purple potatoes!

HEY, FRED.

YOU'VE BEEN THERE, TOO.

UMM. OK.

KEEP IT **REAL**, FREDDY.

GUYS?

BOOP

POOR THING MUST HAVE BEEN LEFT BEHIND BY THE HERD.

THAT'S- THAT'S **NOT** A COW. I DON'T KNOW WHAT IT IS, BUT IT'S **NOT** A COW!

CAN WE KEEP IT?

NO! NO **WAY!** IT'S NOT **OURS** AND IT'S NOT A **COW!**

CAN'T YOU SEE?

IT'S GREEN!

OF COURSE WE CAN. HE'LL MAKE A PERFECT PET.

WEDNESDAY

WHO WANTS A TINY APPLE?

THURSDAY

EXCUSE ME.

GOOD COW.

OK, LILY. THINK. YOU'RE NOT CRAZY. THINK. JUST–

COWS. COWS. COWS DON'T LOOK LIKE THAT. IF THEY JUST SAW A–

THAT'S IT!

DALE'S TOILET READS!

GOTCHA.

A'RIGHT. EVERYBODY, TAKE A LOOK AT—

GUYS?

"WELL, WHAT WAS YOUR *THIRD* WISH?" THE MAN ASKED.

"ISN'T IT *OBVIOUS*? I WISHED MY *HEAD* WAS SHAPED LIKE A *GIANT ORANGE!*"

AHEM!

OH, HI-

UHH-

UMM-

LILY! IT'S *LILY.*

RIGHT. LILY. I KNEW THAT.

WE JUST WENT OUT FOR A QUICK WALK. SORRY WE FORGOT YOU.

YOU'VE BEEN GONE FOR *FIVE* HOURS!

YEAH, SORRY ABOUT THAT-

...

CHAMP.

AAH!

OOF!

OW!

ACK!

SO . . .

ARE YA FRIENDLY?

YES?

OH, WELL *THAT'S* WONDERFUL. LEMME HELP YOU UP.

I'M **KRUGER**, AN' THAT'S MY BROTHER, **DUNNING**. WELCOME TO FLECKOWITZ FARMS.

OK, HI. I'M LILY.

AND I NEED TO ASK YOU ABOUT ONE OF YOUR ANIMALS.

YOU EVER **HEAR** OF CHANGELINGS?

CHANGELINGS?

YEAH, MAGICAL **CREATURES** WHO CAN MAKE YOU **THINK** THEY'RE SOMETHIN' ELSE.

THEY'RE OPPORTUNISTS. THEY **TRICK** THEIR WAY IN AND **PUSH** PEOPLE OUT, EVENTUALLY **REPLACIN'** THEM COMPLETELY.

IT'S AN **ANCIENT** KIND OF MAGIC THAT **MOST** FOLKS THINK AIN'T AROUND NO MORE.

IT WAS OUR **GREAT GRAMPAPPY** WHO STARTED UP THIS FARM, ALMOST THIRTY YEARS AGO, GIVE OR TAKE.

HE **BOUGHT** THE LAND **SIGHT** UN**SEEN** FROM A **MYSTERIOUS STRANGER.** HE SAID NOT BEIN' MORE **CAUTIOUS** WAS JUST ONE OF HIS REGRETS.

'PARENTLY, THOSE **CREATURES** WERE ALREADY HERE WHEN HE **ARRIVED**. CREEPY, GREEN **MONSTERS** ROAMING AROUND ALL OVER THE UPPER FIELDS.

CALLING...
CREEPY
REALTOR

9:49

HE *DIDN'T KNOW* WHAT THEY **WERE** AT FIRST SO HE CALLED UP THE MAN WHO SOLD HIM THE PLACE.

TURNS **OUT** THEY'D BEEN **TRAPPED** HERE AT *BLACK SAND BEACH* SOMEHOW, AS A WAY OF STOPPIN' 'EM FROM INFILTRATING THE ENTIRE HUMAN *RACE*.

NOW **GRAMPS** WAS GONNA JUST *WIPE* 'EM ALL *OUT* AND BE DONE WITH IT, BUT THEN HE DISCOVERED SOMETHING. . .

THEM COOKIN' SMELLED DELICIOUS . . .

SO, FOR TOO MANY GENERATIONS TO COUNT, WE'VE BEEN FARMING THOSE THINGS.

TWICE A YEAR WE HAVE TO SHIFT THE HERD DOWN TO THE LOWER PADDOCK WHILE THE GRASS GROWS BACK UP HERE AND WHAT HAVE YOU.

WE **KNOWED** THAT PEOPLE WOULD GET SCARED IF THEY **SAW** 'EM, SO WE SEND OUT BOXES O'THEM **SLEEPYTATERS** SO NO ONE'D NOTICE.

SO, THE SLEEPYTATERS? THEY'RE–?

JUST REGULAR POTATERS.

EXCEPT THEY WAS **GROWN** IN SOIL FERTILIZED FROM THEM CREATURES' MANURE.

I DON'T KNOW, MAYBE SOME **MAGIC** LEAKED INTO THE DIRT.

THEIR MEAT DON'T SELL SINCE IT'S GREEN, AND THEIR MANURE DON'T SELL BECAUSE IT GLOWS AND MAKES A HUMMIN' SOUND.

IMAGINE THAT.

BUT SEE WE *NOTICED* TATERS, NOT ONLY DID THEY GET ALL *SLEEPY*, THEY **ALSO** STOPPED SEEIN' HOW WEIRD LOOKING THE ANIMALS ARE.

SO WE SEND OUT A BOX TO **ANYONE** WHO LIVES IN THE PATH OF THE **STAMPEDE**, TELL 'EM COWS ARE COMIN' THROUGH AND THEY EITHER **SLEEP** RIGHT THROUGH IT OR THINK THEY SEE *COWS*.

IT'S A PERFECT SYSTEM!

ONE HUNDRED PERCENT FLAWLESS.

WELL, *I* DIDN'T EAT THE SLEEPYTATERS, BUT MY FRIENDS *DID*, AND ONE OF YOUR *HERD* GOT STUCK IN A HAMMOCK AND THEY THOUGHT IT WAS A *COW*, AND NOW THEY THINK IT'S *ME*!

YUP.

THAT IS A PICKLE.

A PICKLE INDEED. AND I CAN'T BELIEVE THEY'RE STILL PRETENDING TO GET STUCK IN HAMMOCKS!

IT'S A CLASSIC *CATCH* TWENTY SOMETHIN' SITUATION. THE TATERS'RE **DANGEROUS**, BUT IN THE *OLD* DAYS IF A CREATURE GOT LOOSE THEY'D DRAG A FELLER OFF AN' BURY HIM TO MAKE THEIR CHARM WORK.

WELL, *ANYWHO—*

THANKS FER STOPPIN' BY. **LET** US KNOW YER NEW ADDRESS IF YOU WANT SOME **DISCOUNT** MEAT.

WAIT? NEW *ADDRESS?* YOU'RE NOT GONNA **HELP** ME? WE *HAVE TO* **STOP** THIS THING!

WE HAVE TO *BREAK THE SPELL!*

OH HUSH. BY **NOW** YOUR OLD FRIENDS DON'T EVEN *RECOGNIZE* YOU. YOU MIGHT AS WELL BE A COMPLETELY DIFFERENT PERSON TO THEM.

PLUS, THERE'S ONLY *ONE* WAY TO BREAK THE SPELL AND IT'S **NEAR** ON IMPOSSIBLE.

THAT *GLAMOUR*, OR WHATEVER YE CALL IT, THE WEIRDO WHAT SOLD PAPPY FLECKOWITZ THE LAND SAID THE **ONLY** WAY TO BREAK IT WAS T'MAKE THE CREATURE LAUGH.

YUP.

APPARENTLY IT'S LAUGH IS *SO* MONSTROUS THAT IT . . .

SNAPS PEOPLE OUT OF IT RIGHT AWAY.

THEN THEY SEE THE CREATURE FOR WHAT IT REALLY IS.

SOUNDS EASY ENOUGH.

SO YOU'D **THINK**. BUT THOSE **HORSEY-HEADED, STOMACH-TOOTHED, TURTLE THINGS** DON'T LAUGH AT REGULAR JOKES.

LEGEND HAS IT THEY ONLY LAUGH AT A JOKE THAT **NO ORDINARY HUMAN** COULD EVER FIND FUNNY.

YOU FIND **THAT JOKE** AND YOU'LL BE BACK WITH YOUR FRIENDS *LICKETY-SPLIT*.

BUT YOU *BETTER* DO IT *FAST*. ONCE THAT GLAMOUR TAKES HOLD PERMANENT LIKE, WELL YOU'RE OUTTA LUCK.

I THINK I HAVE A WAY!

HERE! THIS IS OUR BEST AND CLEANEST SPOON.

EXCELLENT. THIS WILL DO NICELY.

MR. WEST, WOULD YOU MIND DOING ME A FAVOR?

BREATHE SOME HOT AIR ON THIS SPOON AND PRESS IT ON YOUR NOSE.

URR- WHAT'S GOING ON? LILY, WHY ARE YOU IN YOUR PAJAMAS?

WHERE DID THE SPOONSPECTOR GO?

WHAT- WHAT IS THAT THING?

THE END.

Coming in Summer 2021,

the second book in the BLACK SAND BEACH series

Here's the step by step process of creating a page of comic. I try to do as much as possible with pen and paper because I really hate using a computer. Paper just feels nicer to me. The downside is, it's really hard to change anything if your editor doesn't like it, which means you have to work extra hard to make your editors scared of you. For this, I recommend always wearing a ghost costume to meetings.

Page 47:
They all walk in cautiously, looking around. Inside is a spiral staircase leading up to the viewing deck. There's a big metal pole in the center, rusted but smooth. It goes up through the ceiling and into the light mechanism part. It also goes all the way through the floor, through what was once a perfectly fitted hole, but it now a misshapen gap in the wooden floorboards.

Eleanor:
Well, I'd say no one has been in here for a long time. So, if we're thinking that someone was in here turning the light on-

[...]:
[...]n't you say this lighthouse was [...]lly automated.

Eleanor:
Yeah, but I also said it never worked properly.

1: Script
Everyone has a different way of scripting. I switch between excessive descriptions of every panel and nothing but dialogue, with a loose note on what might be going on visually. This page is definitely the latter.

2: Thumbnails
Once the script's written, as messy as it may be, I do thumbnails for every page. This lets me see if the pacing is right or if I'm staying on a scene too long, meaning I have to cram too much in somewhere else.

3: Pencils
Erasing pencils sucks and makes my arm hurt, so I use blue pencils that don't get picked up by scanners. Plus, they look cooler.

Normally I pencil a page then ink it right away, but since this was a new series, I ended up penciling an entire chapter at once, just in case there were any major changes needed. Thanks to my convincing ghost costume, there were not.

4: Lettering
I hate lettering, but I do like how it looks over pencils though, and I do like how it lets me know where I can cut corners on inking and coloring.

5: Inking
The fun part. The part that immediately makes the page look complete. Also the part where you only get one shot, because if you screw it up it's there forever. This is the part where I feel the most like an action hero, because one mistake and I could fall right out of my exploding helicopter.

6: Colors.
Coloring is a strange process. I only started coloring about a year ago and I realized that it can be the easiest or hardest part of making a comic. The actual technical skills you need to learn are very simple, and anyone can be an acceptable colorist, because it really is like a faster version of coloring in. Knowing where the shadows and highlights go, knowing when to use an effect, that's the part that comes from really knowing how to put an image together. This is a pretty cartoony looking book, so the coloring is mostly very simple, but I think any more rendering on these characters would detract from the line work and design.

So, now you know how my comics get made, but the best thing about comics is that you can make them pretty much any way you like. Paint them, scribble them, carve them in a tree, arrange gum you find to make pictures, it really doesn't matter. Just write something and put pictures with it.

ACKNOWLEDGMENTS

First off I want to thank Ray. This book took almost three and a half months to write, draw, and color, and he put up with me throughout like a champ. Late nights on the phone from my office, telling him about the stories and all the little details I was seeding for the rest of the series, waking up early to make me coffee so I could get started again the next day, he did it all.

Lucy Campagnolo and Theo Macdonald, thank you for reading each chapter as it was done to make sure it was scary enough.

I need to thank Jacqueline for helping me maintain my energy levels during some of the most intense drawing sessions of my life.

Paul Wolff offered so much inspiration for these stories with his vast knowledge of electrical circuits and all the science that seems like magic to me. He also tolerated me turning our office into a dorm room, with clothes and blankets strewn about for weeks at a time.

To my friend and roommate, Alex Burke. Thank you for calling me every few days when I didn't come home to make sure I was still alive. Thank you for offering to bring me coffee and for trying to remind me there was an outside world.

I cannot overstate how supportive Bethany Buck has been as an editor or how lucky I am that she and I crossed paths. From the moment I met her, I knew we were going to be friends, and I'm so grateful to have her back in my world.

Vicki Marsdon is the kind of agent everyone should be trying to get. She knows exactly when to let me run wild with a thousand new proposals and when to reign me in because I'm about to land on something wonderful.

Finally, I want to thank Nigel, my best friend, my soulmate, the plastic skeleton I never knew I needed. His permanent smile and dapper outfits remind me what I'm working for.

RICHARD FAIRGRAY

is a writer, artist, and colorist, best known for his work in comic books such as *Blastosaurus* and *Ghost Ghost*, and picture books such as *Gorillas in our Midst, My Grandpa Is a Dinosaur,* and *If I Had an Elephant*. As a child he firmly believed he would grow up and eat all the candy he wanted and stay up as late as he liked. By drawing pictures when he wasn't meant to and reading all the things people told him not to, he has made his dream come true.

Richard now splits his time between Los Angeles and Surrey, British Columbia, where he is able to work furiously, surrounded by plastic skeletons, dogs, friends, loved ones and (possibly) the most comprehensive collection of Courtney Love bootlegs on the planet.